ROLL AGAINST *Trust*

ALLYSON LINDT

ACELETTE PRESS

This book is a work of fiction.

While reference might be made to actual historical events or existing locations, the names, characters, places and incidents are either the product of the author's imagination or are used fictitiously, and any resemblance to actual persons, living or dead, business establishments, events, or locales is entirely coincidental.

Manufactured in the United States of America

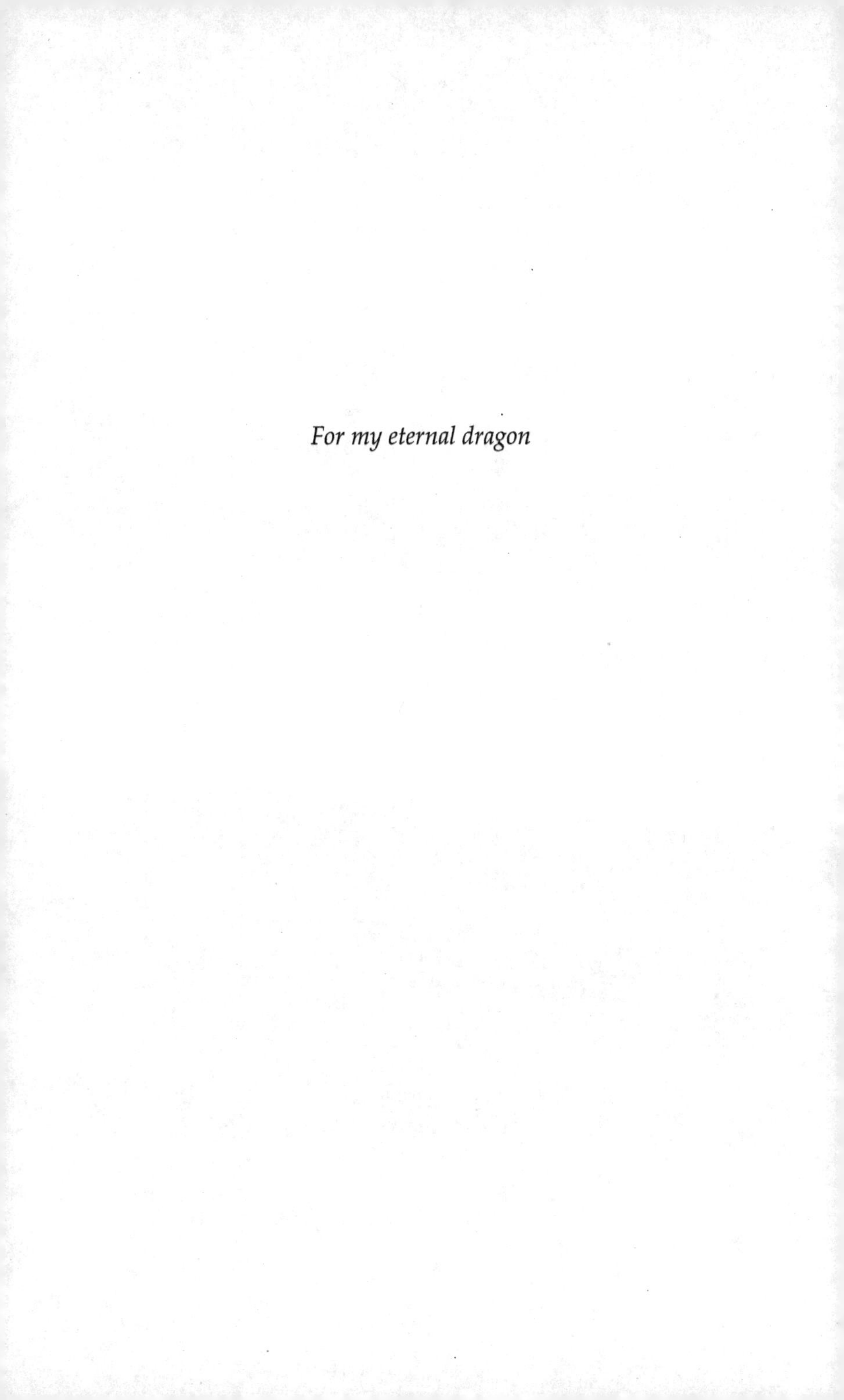

For my eternal dragon

"I'm not sharing a cramped inn room with two orcs, a halfling thief who keeps stealing my panties, and a sweaty paladin. He hasn't taken off that armor in a freaking month."

Ryan draped himself across the couch to lay his head in my lap. Brown eyes so dark they were almost black crinkled at the corners when he laughed up at me. "C'mon, Tash, join me in the bath. We'd save water at the same time, and that kind of conservationism should do something for your druid sensibilities, right?"

"My character's name is Ardra," I corrected him out of habit, not irritation. It had only taken me a couple of weeks of campaigning with him to realize he was just going to use my real name, regardless of whom I was role-playing as. I made a half-hearted attempt to push him upright. "And aren't you supposed to be celibate?"

"Absolutely not. As of now, I serve a god of orgies and wine. Dionysus, maybe?"

Seth looked up from behind his dungeon master screen, eyebrows raised. "He's not in our pantheon." His mouth twisted in thought. "Then again, sure, why the hell not? Roll against your charisma."

I laughed in disbelief. "I'm not taking a bath with him, water conservation or not." Even as the protest passed my lips, my imagination crept in to taunt me. My druid character might prefer the plague over rubbing skin with his paladin, but I wouldn't mind watching Ryan strip down. Or Seth, for that matter.

They were as different in personality as appearance. Ryan was one of the few guys I'd ever met taller than my five-eleven, and he was as thin as a blade. His short hair was the same shade as his almost-black eyes, and his deep voice always sent shivers down my spine.

Seth, on the other hand, was only an inch or so shorter than me. He kept his blond hair in a ponytail, his broad shoulders reflected how dedicated he was to his gym time, and his attention to detail was why we always let him run our Advanced Dungeons & Dragons campaigns.

The two of them lived together—Seth rented a room from Ryan. All three of us had become quick friends when I'd started working for the same company as them about two years earlier. I'd gotten over my crushes on both early in our friendship.

A decision made easier by the fact I'd married and

divorced in my early twenties, and learned from the experience not to trust myself or my partner in a long-term relationship. I was that bad at reading myself and the people around me. But that didn't mean I had a problem with looking. Or, on occasion, letting fantasy run rampant through my thoughts when I was alone and wanted more than just batteries to help the vibrator do its job.

Dice clattered against the table, and Seth let out a sharp, "Ha!" He looked at Ryan. "You've failed to seduce the fair maiden."

"Not even possible." Ryan sat up, frowning at the dice. "I want a re-roll."

"Nope." Seth shook his head. "No mulligans. Pick up a bar wench, or you'll have to hit the sack alone tonight."

If I squinted, I could make out the red letters on the microwave in the kitchen. Almost two a.m. This had become a ritual for the three of us at our weekly role-playing sessions. Even after everyone else threw in the towel and headed home, we'd stay up long into Saturday morning, waiting to see who would fold first and either fall asleep or call it quits. Tonight we'd been sillier than usual, so we'd be here a while longer. I was fine with that. I was enjoying the evening too much to be the person who tapped out.

"I'm not tired," Ryan announced. "So, after my bath, I'm going for a walk in the woods."

Seth looked up at me, pale eyes hauntingly captivating in the dimly lit living room. "Are you going with him, my lady?"

"Forget that. The bath is free. I'm rinsing off the grime."

"Boring!" Ryan winked at me, no malice in his tone. He gestured to himself. "You could have had all this if you hadn't waited."

My gaze traveled over his lithe frame: the way his T-shirt hugged his torso, the jeans with as many tears as fabric. A throb nagged between my legs, accompanied by a brief flash of letting him strip me down and joining him in an actual bath. I nudged the daydream aside to save for later, trying to keep my expression neutral. "I'll live. I'm sure."

"All right, mister 'bath time is boring now'." Seth tapped his pencil against the table. "What are you doing in the forest that's more interesting?"

Ryan shrugged. "I'm alone for the first time in a month. I've left all my mates in the inn room or bath. I'm jerking off."

Heat flooded my skin thanks to the enticing mental image of freeing Ryan's erection from his torn jeans and stroking his shaft, and I was grateful it was dark in the room.

Seth snorted with laughter. "Roll against your stealth."

Ryan was so screwed. He hadn't put any points into dexterity. Said there was no reason for finesse when he could kill anything with his massive sword.

"What? Why? I left my armor in the room," Ryan protested.

"And you're a klutz even without it. Roll."

Ryan tossed the dice and groaned at the result. "Damn it."

Seth shot me a look I couldn't interpret, and scribbled some notes on the pad in front of him. "You find a nice, empty clearing in the forest, and start to beat one out. Our lovely druid, Ardra, is almost done with her bath when she hears a disconcerting noise outside. She grabs her dressing gown, and races to investigate."

"I don't get dressed first?"

Seth smirked. "No. And you don't hide, or check for traps, or anything else. The only thing out there is the mighty paladin, Galahad."

If there had been anyone else still around, or I hadn't been silly tired and a little turned on, I might have argued that if I already knew who was out there, I wouldn't need to go investigate. But giddiness, and the daydream-induced dampness between my legs, let boldness have its reign. "All right, I'll go investigate."

"You rush through the small patch of woods behind the inn, dressing gown threatening to tear free on the wild growth, and stumble to a stop at the edge of a small clearing, agape at what you see."

I made a flash of decision and rushed forward with my response before I could talk myself out if it. If we were going to role-play this ridiculous scenario, and neither of them was going to balk, I wanted details. "Which is…?"

When Ryan met my gaze this time, something dangerous laced his teasing expression. "Just because I couldn't have you in the bath doesn't mean I'm not fantasizing about it. I'm leaning against a nearby tree, breeches around my ankles, and cock in my hand."

I liked this. Dampness grew in my panties. "And I'm properly impressed. The paladin is well hung."

"Roll against getting caught." Seth's command blended into the delicious tension in the room instead of destroying it.

My ability to move silently through the forest was higher than Ryan's charisma. There was no way I was risking staying hidden in the shadows. I let my impulse continue to drive. "No need. I'm so shocked and compelled by what I see, I gasp and step into the clearing for a better look."

A wicked smile tugged up the corner of Ryan's mouth, and I swore he looked like a big bad wolf about to devour me. In the most delicious and ravenous way possible. "Your appearance catches me off guard, but I've never minded putting on a show. I slow down when I realize your gown has fallen open. It drapes off your tits, and shows me a perfect patch of red fuzz hiding in the V between your legs."

A teeny tiny part of me said I should correct him. I hated my copper-colored hair, so my character was blonde. I wasn't interrupting this, though. In the dim room, with just our voices and his captivating eyes, I could slip into the fantasy we were painting, and it had me wet. "I stare as you stroke up and down. I've never seen such an impressive man before."

"I don't have to be doing this alone, you know." He licked his bottom lip. "You're welcome to join me. I bet the trees you usually fuck don't spread you open the way I would."

There were times when Ryan's direct comments embarrassed me. Now wasn't one of them. "I'm too dumbstruck to leave. I can't stop thinking about letting you have your way with me."

"I close the distance between us in just a few steps, and nudge your robe farther to the side, exposing one fleshy, soft breast. I glide my hand up your ribs, cupping the mound, and dragging a callused thumb over your already rock-hard nipple."

My own nubs twinged in response, aching under my bra as the phantom touch flicked over one. "I let out a soft moan and step closer until your…" I fumbled for a moment. Could I actually talk like this out loud? In the context of the game, yes. "Until your manhood presses into my leg."

His dark stare held me captive now. Watching his lips move as he painted his character's desires. Hearing his seductive voice. "I squeeze and pinch at the pink temptation in my hand, and you squirm under the attention. I trace my mouth down your chest, dropping to my knees as I move to your stomach. My fingers part your pussy. My gods you're wet.

I flick my tongue out, and groan at your incredible taste."

Oh gods was right. My thighs squeezed together at the thought of him buried between my legs, licking. "I whimper and tangle my fingers in your hair. This sensation is new and incredible."

"I trace ancient runes over your clit with my tongue as I slide two fingers inside you. You're tight, but slippery. I want you wrapped around my cock before the end of the night. I lick and suck, letting your gasps guide me while I finger fuck you."

This was the single most erotic fantasy I'd ever delved into, and I knew it was because it was all vocal and shared. Something was even more arousing about the fact Seth was still listening to us, and not interrupting. I wanted to be riding Ryan by the end of the night, too. Err, my character did. "You're good at this. Apparently there's some truth to the rumors the village girls spread between each town."

He smirked. "They spread more than rumors. But none of them taste as incredible as you do. You're intoxicating. I devour your pussy, nipping with my teeth as you get more vocal. I want you to come."

I might just from his words. Not really, but maybe. "I'm so close. You hit a spot inside and pleasure explodes through me. I clench around your fingers until my legs are weak and everything is too sensitive to touch. But I want more."

"I help you sink to your knees and sit on the ground in front of you, dick harder than it's ever been and standing at attention. I wonder what your perfect, full lips would feel like wrapped around my cock, but I can't wait for that. I know how soaked you are and I need you riding me. Your pale skin is flushed as you straddle me. With one hand on your hips and the other on my rod, I guide you into place. I want to take this bit slow, but your heat is too tempting. I thrust up, plunging inside you."

I almost arched my back at the thought of him impaling me. My panties were soaked, and I was going to see this through. Wanted him—his paladin, whatever—to come hard because of me. "You're so big it hurts, and I love it. I try and measure your pace by rocking up and down slowly against you."

"I want to stretch this moment out. I glide my hands up your chest, cupping your perfect tits and thumbing your nipples. Your skin is gorgeous in the full moon."

A new voice interrupted the conversation, but Seth's smooth tone wasn't jarring. It added to the dreamlike quality of the entire moment. "The two of you have made too much noise and the innkeeper is coming to check and make sure everything is all right. He hesitates at the edge of the clearing, dumbstruck and amazed at the scene before him. He's instantly hard at the sight of two bodies intertwined with each other, panting and glistening."

2

If I had been turned on before, it was nothing compared to what ratcheted through me at the new arrival. My fantasies had always been about one or the other of them, never both men. I didn't know which I liked more, the thought of Seth getting off by watching us, or the idea he might join in. "Are you simply a passive observer?"

Ryan gripped his leg hard enough I saw the cords and muscles in his arm strain in the dim light, still watching me. "I see the curious interloper over your shoulder, and slide my hands to your back. Raking down your spine, I cup your ass and pull your upper body forward, never letting up on the steady rhythm. I want to pound you hard and fast, but I think you want this more."

Seth picked up the dialog without hesitation. "I drop my breeches as I join you in the clearing. I kneel behind you, and you jump then sigh when I run my hand down your perfect ass. I slip my fingers between your legs from behind, amazed at how incredible you feel. I stroke his cock while I coat my hand in your juices."

I hid a wince. Please don't let that ruin it. Seth was bisexual, and Ryan was as straight as I had ever seen. But the slip in narration didn't break things up. I didn't even know if I could speak at this point. My mouth was dry with anticipation. I didn't have to worry about coming up with a response, though.

"I use your arousal to lube my dick." Seth's voice wasn't as deep, but it still had a hypnotic effect. "I nudge your ass with the head, and in your almost frenzied state, you let me in with little resistance.

Both of them inside me at the same time? My hands twitched and I forced them not to actually move to my breasts and pleading clit. "Gods, this is amazing."

"Filling you with two hard, thick cocks has made you even tighter," Ryan said. "I finger your clit, and you almost come from the contact. As you lean forward, I raise my head up to suck on one of those exhilarating pink nubs that's taunting me. Taking it between my teeth, I nibble and flick at it with my tongue."

"I won't last long," I manage to keep the breathlessness out of my voice. It was true. If we did this much longer, I might not be able to keep my hands out of my pants. Or theirs.

"Your enraptured shouts milk me better than your

tight hole," Ryan said. "And as you come a second time, I pound you hard. I grunt at the feelings, and spurt deep inside you when I climax."

"I pull out," Seth added. "Beating my cock, stroking it when I watch the two of you grind, and cover your backside with my orgasm."

"We all collapse on top of each other, spent." There was a hint of strain to Ryan's voice. "After we catch our breath, none of us says anything. We extract ourselves from each other and make our way back to the inn for some of the best sleep we've had in months."

A silence descended on the room. Had we just made a mistake? Were they actually imagining me in that scene the way I had with them, or had this just been a random game?

"Okay, then." Seth finally shattered the still. "Wow. Fortunately, the druid is protected by her gods, and we don't have to deal with pregnancy during this raiding party."

"Good call." Ryan sank back into the cushions with a small exhale.

And just like that, the moment was over. We laughed and joked a little more, but it wasn't much longer before one of them—I wasn't even sure who, or maybe it was both—decided to call it a night.

"It's too late for you to drive home, Tasha." Seth disappeared from the room and returned moments later with a pillow and blanket. "Stay here."

I wasn't going to argue. It was as common as

anything for me to crash on Ryan and Seth's couch. I made up my temporary bed, and they said their good nights.

As the house fell silent, sleep evaded me. I stared at the ceiling, images still teasing me, and unresolved need still begging for my attention. Were they both asleep yet? I listened to the house creak, wondering if each new noise was one of them getting up.

I slid a hand under my shirt, hidden by the blanket, and pinched my nipple. I had to bite my lip to keep from letting out a groan of pleasure.

I tweaked and pulled harder, letting snippets of the off-course game roll through my mind. My other hand slid down, unbuttoned my jeans, and dipped under my panties. I really was wet.

I stroked myself slowly, trying to draw out the moment. Something creaked, like footsteps, and I froze, breath catching in my throat. The noise paused nearby. Would they know I wasn't asleep? Was I breathing too loud? Not loud enough?

Would I prefer to get caught, and let whichever of them it was watch, and maybe help? I liked that idea. My clit trembled in response. Seconds later the footsteps resumed, and I heard the bathroom door swing shut. A faint light moved a few inches across the other side of the room, but petered out before it reached me.

A soft grunting drifted toward my ears. I couldn't tell which of them it was, but heat and arousal burned through me when I realized it was the sound of one of them jerking off.

Knowing I wasn't the only one impacted, and part of me hoping to get caught, I resumed my self-attentions. I closed my eyes and let the faint sound from the bathroom penetrate my fantasy. I stroked my swollen button as I imagined Ryan pushing himself deep inside me, while Seth watched, stroking his own cock.

The sounds from the bathroom increased in pace and volume, and so did my masturbation. I was so close. I worked myself faster, moving my other hand from my tit to slide two fingers inside me. The penetration was enough to push me over the edge, and I arched my back as I came.

Seconds later, the grunts from the bathroom grew more frantic and then abruptly stopped. The toilet flushed, the footsteps crossed the room, and a bedroom door closed.

I sank back onto the couch, mentally and physically spent, and drifted into a solid sleep.

I NEEDED COFFEE IN A SERIOUS WAY. WHO MADE PEOPLE come into the office at six-thirty for a conference call? Besides my boss, apparently. I had a laptop, a cell phone, and a perfectly good pair of PJ's no one would have noticed I was wearing. I could have taken the call from home just fine.

In contrast to when I'd arrived an hour and a half ago, all the lights on the floor were on now, and people were filling the desks. I rubbed my eyes to try and wake myself up as I wove through the maze of cubicles back to my own.

The one nice thing about the early meeting had been that it took my mind off what happened over the weekend with Seth and Ryan. It was just a spontaneous thing, but ever since Friday night, fantasy and images had teased me, most of them involving being pinned between both guys, and feeling hands in more places at once than should have been possible. The reminder sent heat rushing through me, and an insistent throb echoed between my legs.

Now was definitely not the time to be entertaining those thoughts. Not in the middle of the office, knowing the entire thing had been a game to both of them. Especially after I'd run out of the house this morning without any makeup and no time to do anything with my out-of-control curls besides pull them back and hope my hair didn't frizz. I just wasn't feeling the sexy those fantasies required.

I dropped into my chair with a heavy sigh, but a trace of my exhaustion vanished when I went to log into my computer. A cup of coffee sat in front of my keyboard, with TASHA scrawled on the sleeve in Seth's familiar block-letter handwriting. Above my name was a pair of horns, with a halo falling off one. Despite my Monday morning grumbles, a smile overtook my face. He didn't always do things like that, but he'd known I had an unreasonably early meeting today. Maybe everything was back to normal between us after all.

I sent him a quick thank you over messenger, wishing I had time for more chatting. But there were deadlines to meet, and clients to please. I had only officially been a project manager for about six months, and this was my first solo assignment. So far, everything was going smoothly, and I intended to keep it that way. I dove into double-checking the project milestones to make sure we were on track, and quickly lost myself in time.

My cell phone rang, and after a brief glance at the "Unknown Number", I ignored it. I'd learned too much from years of fighting off bill collectors for debts my ex-husband had raked up in my name. One of the big lessons was to never take those calls in the office, especially during months I couldn't afford another payment.

I dropped back into what I was doing. The morning noise faded into the background as I worked.

"Hey, Tash." Ryan's greeting dragged me back to the here and now, and his playful tug on my ponytail sent an unexpected, but pleasant, flicker of want through me.

A brief image flashed in my head of him pulling my hair hard while he slid inside me from behind. I banished the thought before my panties could get too damp, and spun to face him. "Morning."

He pulled up a nearby chair, and dropped into it.

He studied me for a minute. The attention lasted long enough for concern to flit in. Had I spilled coffee on my sweater? Did I look that bad without any mascara and eyeliner?

"You look good today." A grin broke his serious expression. "It's the blue top with your eyes or something."

"Thanks." The compliment caught me off-guard and heat rushed under my skin. He was just being polite, right? Not like I was going to ask for clarification. I'd take the compliment for what it was. "What's up?"

His brows furrowed for a moment, then his casual demeanor slipped back in, and his voice dropped in volume. "Kitner says Zedophap has an issue with their config."

It might have sounded like a secret code to anyone else, but to me, Mark Kitner was in senior management and in charge of our department, Zedophap was the client account I was managing, and as the business analyst on the project, Ryan was in charge of working with them to make sure we configured our product to their specifications. And I knew for a fact, after that morning's phone call, there were no issues or concerns. "Nope. You're clear."

"You're the best." He hopped to his feet. "You joining me and Seth for lunch today?"

"Only if we go somewhere fast."

"You'd enjoy it a lot more if we took our time." He

trailed his fingers lightly along the back of my neck, sending pleasant tremors racing over my skin.

My nipples tightened at the light touch, and my belly clenched. It took every ounce of my restraint not to lean into the teasing gesture with a sigh. This kind of joking wasn't new for us. I needed to bring my hormones under control. "I'll see what I can do."

"Killer." He gave my ponytail a final tug, and seconds later dropped into his own cube.

As I shifted in my seat to get back to work, the lace of my bra slid across my breasts, making my nipples harder. How had that one little moment turned me on so much?

"Natasha." Mark's sharp tone squashed my growing arousal. "Do you have a few minutes?"

I'd always hated that question, especially when it came from my boss. If I said I had time, did that mean I wasn't working hard enough? But if I said I was busy, would it sound like a brush off? Besides, its vague nature frequently meant bad things. I always just settled for, "What did you need?"

He nodded into his office. "It'll be fast."

That sounded bad. Mark waited until I was seated in one of the chairs across from his desk, before closing the door and taking his own seat. He clucked his tongue against the roof of his mouth. "We have an issue."

Shit. I let my concern leak onto my face. "With Zedophap?"

He nodded. "I just got off the phone with their VP

of marketing. Apparently, they started doing some basic user acceptance testing first thing this morning, and nothing is working like they want it to."

A million possibilities raced through my head. Bad programming, poor data entry, mismanaged client expectations. Where to start? Oh, right. "They said on the call everything was going fine."

He sighed and leaned forward, forearms resting on the edge of his desk, and fingers interlocked. "That's part of the problem." His tone was grave, and his forehead bunched into wrinkles. "They're not comfortable bringing this up with you, because they say you haven't handled their concerns in the past."

My stomach clenched, and indignation rose inside me. I tempered it as best I could. "I didn't know there was anything outstanding."

"When I gave you this job, I warned you that a project manager has to be the bad guy sometimes."

I remembered that conversation distinctly. As I sat in front of him now, racking my brain, I couldn't think of why that was relevant. "You did."

"If there's someone on this team who's not pulling their weight, I need to know."

My insides wrenched a little more. Did he have someone specific in mind? "As far as I know, everyone's doing great."

He sighed, and looked at his hands for a moment before meeting my gaze again. "I'm trying to be polite about this, Natasha. This is a big client, and we can't afford to lose them. I understand working as a team, and camaraderie and all that. I'm not asking you to hang someone out to dry with the client, but if you're having an issue, and you can't deal with it, you need to tell me who's causing the problem."

He took a deep breath, eyes never leaving mine. "If we lose Zedophap—if they do something like sue us for breach of contract—someone is going to lose their job. I don't want it to be you if you're not at fault. If it's someone else, and we can fix this now, I'd rather do that. I don't want to have to let anyone go."

I swallowed the bile rising in my throat. I might have wondered how idle the threat was, but I'd seen it happen before on botched implementations. The bigger issue was I didn't know what was wrong. How was I supposed to discipline someone if I didn't see a problem? "I understand."

"I knew you would. I'll forward you their email. Let's track this down quickly and deal with it quietly."

"Yeah. Completely."

His smile returned, and he turned to his computer. "Thanks for your time."

I was numb as I headed back to my desk. I was already living on floated checks and past-due promises. I couldn't afford to lose my job. There had to be a way to make things right. Someone must be overreacting. I'd find the problem, we'd deal with it, and everything would be fine.

I opened Mark's email as soon as I sat down. For the next few hours, I pored through everything related to the complaints, and my chest ached more and more as I dug. All indicators pointed to Ryan. And it wasn't just a little screw-up. It was jaw-dropping, contract-violating, facing-off-a-beholder-who-just-decided-to-tentacle-fuck-us huge.

I didn't want to have this conversation. I didn't have a choice.

3

"Ready for lunch?" Seth stopped on the other side of my chest-high cubicle, resting his arms on top.

My stomach growled in response, and I mentally told it to shut up. I didn't have time for lunch. Maybe I shouldn't have said yes to Ryan's invite so easily this morning. Then again, when I'd talked to him I hadn't known my work world was imploding. I opened my mouth to tell them to go without me.

"You have to eat." Ryan slid into the empty spot next to Seth. "Vending machine food doesn't count."

Then again, maybe this would be the perfect chance to ask him what was going on with Zedophap. We could lessen the sting over food and then fix everything when we got back. The snippet of a plan didn't completely ease my tension, but it helped. I grabbed my purse and locked my computer. "I'm in. Where we going?"

"Fresh Mex," Seth said as we made our way toward the elevators. "Fish taco day."

Ryan snorted. I rolled my eyes. We all joked and laughed as we walked across the street to the dive that made some of the best food anywhere near the office. Any lingering doubt I'd had about things being awkward after our vocal session over the weekend evaporated.

We were all predictable with our orders. Seth would get the daily special, Ryan would want a smothered-pork burrito, and I always opted for the tortilla soup—cheap and hearty enough to get me through the day without starving. They let me order first. I handed over my debit card. A twitch throbbed behind my eye when the cashier swiped it, waited a few seconds and then frowned.

She gave me a nervous smile. "Sorry. Let me try again."

There was nothing to worry about. It was just a register screw-up, it would be—

She handed the card back to me. "I'm sorry. It's declined. Do you want to pay some other way?"

Shit. I gave her my most confident smile, and rifled through my purse, pretending to look for cash I knew wasn't there. It had only been a couple of days since payday. I'd just dropped my rent check off that morning, so there was no way that had cleared yet, and even if it had, I should have had plenty of money left. Embarrassment mingled with my creeping panic.

A hand rested on my shoulder, the familiar heat

drawing me from my spiraling thoughts. "I've got it." Ryan's whisper was barely loud enough for my ears. His voice returned to regular volume. "We're together."

I gave him a grateful smile as we staked out an empty table and waited for Seth. "I'll pay you back. I don't know what happened. I just have to call my bank. Thank you so mu—"

"Don't worry about it." He cut me off before my panic made me ramble out of control. "Chill. Enjoy your lunch. We're even."

"You all right?" Seth asked as he dropped into the empty seat, and set his order number on the edge of the table next to ours.

I forced a smile into place. I wasn't discussing my money problems with either of them. It had taken me months to even tell them I'd been married once upon a time. "Typical Monday, you know? Sucky here and there and everywhere. It'll pass."

Seth studied me, pale eyes trying to pry into my soul, and I turned my attention to chasing the ice in my drink with my straw. A heavy silence fell over the table. Someone set our food in front of us, but I was too distracted to dive in. I needed to ask Ryan about the Zedophap project. Just spit it out.

"Split the difference?" Ryan cut into my hesitation, even though the words triggered an instinct that told me he wasn't talking to me.

Seth took a moment to respond. "He is pretty cute."

Irritation crawled under my skin. Great. Not this. I followed their gazes toward a couple on the other side of the room. She was short and curvy with straight, blonde hair—basically the exact opposite of my physical appearance. He was okay. Not gorgeous, but better than average, and so immaculately dressed I wondered if his T-shirt was pressed. They were scowling at each other in some sort of silent-argument, death-match-stare-down.

The point of Ryan and Seth's *split the difference* was to find an arguing couple, be the friendly stranger with a shoulder to cry on, and if they did things right, Ryan would go home with her number, and Seth with his. My aggravation bubbled up, carried by the tensions of the day. "Could you two not do this? Just this once? Could you maybe let the arguing couples of the world try and work things out on their own for the day?" I winced at the edge in my own voice. *Way to blow things out of proportion, me.*

Two heads whirled in my direction. Seth studied me, brows furrowed. "Are you sure you're okay?"

Ryan's eyes narrowed and he turned back to his food. "Hormonal."

That single word, even though a tiny part of me knew he was teasing, broke something inside. I let out a soft growl and turned my attention to him. I adored everything he did for me, and I felt bad snipping at him since he'd just saved me at the cash register, but sometimes it was as if he just didn't pay attention. Which, now that I thought about it, had to have been what happened at work. "What's going on with Zedophap?"

His jaw opened and then snapped shut again, and his brow furrowed. "Um… stuff? You tell me. You're in charge and you said nothing was wrong."

Not helpful. "Except apparently their configuration is completely screwed up." I didn't want to handle things so aggressively. I needed to dial it back, but the morning had destroyed a portion of my control. I had to fix this. I couldn't lose my job.

"You told me this morning they were cool. Also, not even possible." He turned his attention back to his food. "I double and triple checked. Everything is in order."

And now he was brushing me off. More of my hesitation evaporated, replaced with annoyance. "Are you sure?"

He finally gave me his full attention. "You don't trust me?" A sliver of hurt lingered behind his stare.

I pulled my gaze away first. How could those dark eyes fill me with so much guilt over something that wasn't my fault? This wasn't getting me anywhere. How was I supposed to fix it if he wouldn't even own the problem? Frustration and ambivalence clawed at my skull, making my head ache. I stared at my soup, not daring to focus on anything else. "Just forget it."

"Oh, sure. You throw my reassurances back in my face, and I should just forget it?"

"Something's definitely wrong." Seth cut into the tension.

I whirled on him. "You think?" I shouldn't be taking this out on him at all. I needed to stop now. But worry was gnawing my gut alive. If Ryan didn't take responsibility, my job was at risk. I could fix the problems, but I couldn't hang him out to dry. I also couldn't let it happen again. I dropped my face into my hands. Gods this bit. "Did I mention the sucky Monday bullshit?"

"But you were a little scarce on the details." Seth scooted his chair closer, and tilted his face until it was under mine. "Boo."

A smile slipped out without my permission at his antics. "I'll fix it. It's not a big deal." I didn't know how I'd do it, but this conversation wasn't getting me anywhere.

"You sure?" He traced a line up the top of my leg, drawing away some of my tension. The light contact teased me with ideas that had nothing to do with fixing the issues at work. Of working off all this stress by finding a hidden corner with him. Of letting those skilled fingers roam over me.

What was wrong with me? Lusting after both of them in a single day like this. And still I couldn't stop staring into Seth's pale eyes.

A loud screech cut through the moment, chair legs sliding on tile against their will. "I have to get back to work." Ryan was on his feet. He only looked at me for a moment, jaw set. "Apparently, I'm not doing something right."

The accusation in his tone pulled out my guilt. "I didn't mean—"

"Yeah, you did."

Damn it. I slouched in my chair. I knew his temper well enough to realize I couldn't go after him right now. I looked at Seth again. "Can you pin him down long enough for me to apologize later?"

His smile vanished, too. His, "sure," was flat.

Now what? I rolled the last few minutes through my thoughts, and while it was true I'd started to lash out at Seth, I'd reeled that in quickly.

And then, just as quickly as it had appeared, his sour expression evaporated. "You know I will. Besides, we're going to that thing tonight. He's not going to miss it, and you can apologize then."

"Thing…?" We didn't do stuff on Monday nights.

"OT?"

Original trilogy. That jogged my memory loose. I couldn't believe I'd forgotten about it. A local movie theater was doing screenings of the extended edition Star Wars movies, one a night, all week long. They were showing them in the order they'd been released, instead of in the order of the stories. The tickets had been expensive, so I'd had to pick which one I wanted to see. We'd agreed on Episode IV. Ryan had offered to pick up the rest for me, but I couldn't let him do that. The reminder tugged in more guilt and confusion over what just happened.

Seth nudged me with his shoulder. "I can't believe you forgot."

"I guess I'm more distracted than I realized."

He moved his chair even closer. "Turn. Back toward me."

Curious, but not in any kind of mood to argue, I did what he said. When his fingers dug into my shoulders, a soft groan slipped from my throat.

"You need to chill." His voice was soft. He kneaded away the tension. "You're so tight."

The innuendo-laden words, combined with his warm breath against the back of my neck, slid under my skin, and tempted me. When I closed my eyes, I could picture the vivid scene we'd painted on Friday night. Or better, I could wrap myself in what was happening now and take it a step further. Imagining his hands sliding lower. Cupping my breasts. Pinching my nipples through lace while he sucked on my shoulder.

Wetness pooled between my legs as his fingers dug deeper, and the fantasy grew more detailed.

I forced my eyes open and tried to pull away without jerking out of his touch. I couldn't do this with either one of them. I couldn't destroy friendships because I was daydreaming about guys who didn't see me as anything more than a gaming buddy. I pushed back from the table. "I should get back. I have so much waiting for me."

"No worries. I've got stuff to do too." His smile looked forced. Or I wanted it to. I must be projecting. I knew from experience how horrible I was at reading men.

We were halfway back to the office, neither of us saying much of anything, when my stomach growled and reminded me I'd completely ignored my food. It was a tiny thing, but it was enough to pull all my frustration back to the surface. What was I going to do? About Seth and Ryan, about work, about money? About anything.

When I got back to my desk, my work and cell phone showed twin missed calls. I would have suspected an overambitious bill collector, but there were voicemails to go along with them. It took me a minute to recognize the number, and my gut sank.

I dialed into my cell phone quickly, any thoughts of missed lunch evaporating as I listened to the message. My landlord wanted me to know she'd called to verify funds on my rent check, and was told I couldn't cover it. I muttered every curse I knew as I wandered toward a more private part of the building, already calling my bank.

My balance was twenty-two cents? What the hell? Yes, to speak to a teller. I tried deep breaths to calm myself as the phone rang. It wasn't a big deal. I'd find out it was a data entry error. My money was still there, right? My gut turned in on itself, already knowing better than my head that I wouldn't be that lucky.

Someone finally answered, and I swear my heart leaped into my throat. I gave her my name and account number. "I need to find out what this twelve-hundred dollar withdrawal is on my checking account."

"Sure, I can help with that." Her cheer set my teeth on edge. Keys clacked over the phone, and she made a couple of "hmm" sounds. "Can I have you hold for a minute?"

"Uh, sure?"

She had to answer a question for someone else, right? It wasn't anything to do with me. There was no hold music. Just a click that echoed over the line every fifteen seconds or so. Which, I decided after too many of them, was definitely worse.

"Natasha?" My chest almost exploded when she came back on the line. "Sorry about that. I had to double-check something."

"Of course." I couldn't keep the strain from my voice. "Is everything all right?"

"It looks like the withdrawal is an electronic debit from a First Check Central."

One of his post-dated checks. Shit. In the case of judgments, at least I got a warning, and lawyers tended to be easier to deal with than bill collectors, as long as I was willing to pay something.

But with the post-dated check places, since the check was the collateral, their contract allowed them to go directly to the bank account for their money if they didn't get paid. I just hadn't expected any of those loans to still be outstanding.

I wanted to scream and yell and toss out every vulgar word in existence. But it wasn't her fault. Goddamn my ex. "Can you give me the number of who it came from?"

"Sure. But we can't reverse the charge."

"No, of course not. I understand."

I scrambled to find a pen and paper in my purse, and wrote down the information she gave me. Panic welled up inside. I was broke, I didn't get paid for almost two weeks, and my rent was already late. Did I have enough ramen and macaroni and cheese in the house to eat until payday?

I leaned against a nearby wall and forced myself to not lose it. Freaking out wasn't going to help me. I grasped for strands of reason and broke the problem down logically. What bills could I shift to next paycheck?

Things would be tight, and I couldn't eat out for a few weeks, but I could make the money balance. I could plead with my landlord. I could get an extension on my next car payment. Hopefully.

I made my way back to my desk, rolling the better parts of my plan over and over in my head, certain I could make this work. As long as I didn't linger too long on the not so great bits of my idea—like missing a couple of meals and skipping the coffee—it felt like I had a solution.

I hadn't even had a chance to sit yet when Mark poked his head out of his office and caught my eye. "You have a minute?"

Something told me I didn't want to have this conversation. But it wasn't as if I had a choice. My paycheck was the only thing keeping me from living on the streets, and even then only barely. Speaking of, I still needed to call my landlord. Beg her for more time. She was kind, but I also knew she was tired of my excuses.

The situation jumbled in my head as I made myself comfortable in Mark's office. Solutions and problems and two weeks of cheap starch-for-meals taunted me. I had a jar of change, right? It had only been a couple of months since I cashed it out, but there were probably ten or twenty bucks of coins in there. I could buy oatmeal and some other basics.

"I need to know what's happening with Zedophap." Mark's severe tone dragged me back to the now, and I realized the door was closed once again. Whatever this was, he didn't want eavesdroppers.

At least I had an answer to this. Mostly. "I've got it under control," I assured him. "I know where the issue happened, and I'm putting steps in place to make sure we can resolve it and still meet our milestones." My gaze drifted absentmindedly to a stack of papers on his desk. I tended to read whatever was there upside-down, just to see if it was interesting. It was a habit I always felt bad about, but had never managed to break.

This definitely ranked on the interesting scale. It was a copy of our configuration document, but not the one Ryan had handed to me. Even at a glance, I could tell it was so different from Ryan's, there was no way things would have worked the way the client expected.

He nodded at his monitor, and the email on the screen. "I'm afraid it's more serious than that."

He had to be kidding me. Was this the universe's day to shit on me? "How did we go from fine on the call this morning to more serious than just making things right?"

He shifted the papers around on his desk, sliding the curious document underneath other things, but not before I caught the name of a different business analyst up top. So odd.

"Their legal contacted us. They're talking about arbitration and possible breach of contract."

Whoa. That didn't happen. Not in a single day for sure. People tossed the threat around all the time, but no one acted on it. "What do we do?"

"Do you know where the breakdown happened?"

"It was Ryan, but we're fixing it." The words tumbled out as I dug through my thoughts for solutions. "We can show them an updated timeline by the end of the day. If I talk to the data group, they'll put in a couple extra hours to make sure the existing issues are fixed." I hated to call in that kind of favor from Seth, but I knew he'd help me out. I'd have to owe him a drink. Sometime next year.

I just didn't know why Ryan had so seriously dropped the ball. "No one's losing their jobs, right?"

Mark's face pinched. "I hope not. But your group isn't the only team that's had problems with this account. Marketing hasn't delivered, the call center made promises they can't possibly keep. You need to know how critical this is. And I should warn you, it's not usually the 'grunts' who take the heat for things like this. Since you're managing this part of the implementation, if layoffs happen…"

It would be my head on the chopping block. I didn't need him to finish. "I get it. I'm on it, I promise."

My feet felt like they were boxed in concrete as I trudged out of Mark's office. I had a plan. I could make it all work. As long as I told myself that over and over, there was no room in my head for doubt.

Ryan looked up from his desk when I crossed the room, but I couldn't meet his gaze. And I still needed to call my landlord. Damnit damnit damnit damnit damnit.

I couldn't get ahold of my landlord, so I left her a rambling, probably convoluted, explanation-apology-plea-for-forgiveness, and hoped for the best. Fortunately, we'd bought the Star Wars tickets months earlier. I considered scalping mine but decided instead to give myself one last luxury. I got to enjoy the show on the big screen, surrounded by fans who cheered when the opening text scrolled, and hushed the moment the THX logo grew quiet, the way Lucas intended.

By the time the movie ended, it was almost midnight, and most of the stress of the day had slipped to the back of my mind. I could deal with it all in the morning. There was nothing I could do before tomorrow except enjoy the night.

We stayed through the closing credits, and were some of the last people to leave the theater. My philosophy at the movies was if we had been in a rush, we wouldn't be there. Waiting a couple extra minutes meant we didn't have to fight traffic leaving the parking lot. Not that there would be much tonight. This had been the latest showing in the place, and while the theater had been packed, it was still just one out of twenty-four.

Our conversation was casual as we pushed out a side door, and more of my stress ebbed. Whatever weird tension had happened at lunch was in the past. We joked and talked as we made our way to the far corner of the parking lot. Seth liked to park way out there because...well, he said it was because it wouldn't hurt us to walk. But I knew it was more because his BMW was his baby, and he felt like it was safer away from the other cars.

As we drew closer, the darkness closed in around us, and I realized the parking lot lights in the entire section were out. "Ooh, dark and creepy. What if there are bad things hiding in the shadows?"

"Don't worry, we'll protect you." Ryan tossed an arm around my shoulder, his voice sliding into the same false bravado he used when he was playing his paladin.

It was just a friendly gesture, like so many hundreds he'd made before. But the part of my mind that had been out of control all day honed in on the warm contact. The familiar security and at the same time, bold assumption in the gesture. I was too drained from the day to completely suppress my response. I teased back, "What if you're the big-bad I need protecting from?"

We'd reached the car, and there was no one else nearby. All the other filmgoers were parked far enough away their voices barely reached us. Even then, most of them were already gone.

"You've got a good point." Seth grabbed my wrists loosely and tugged them behind my back. I could have broken away if I wanted, but the heat of his palms against my skin held me captive more than his grip. His hot words caressed the back of my neck. "It's dark enough no one will see us."

I didn't want to hold back the fantasies. Need coursed through me, driving my response. "So what's to stop you from taking advantage of the situation?"

Ryan stepped closer, pinning me between the two. "Only you."

Hesitation wormed up inside. These were my two best friends. Even if I had been dreaming about Ryan yanking my hair and screwing me hard, or Seth sliding his fingers inside me, it didn't mean I was willing to surrender our current bond over it. "I still have to look you in the eye in the morning."

"That wasn't a problem after Friday night." Seth's lips glided over my skin.

A whimper slipped from my throat, and my heart threatened to hammer out of my chest. "That was just a game."

"So's this." Ryan traced a finger over my bottom lip, and my mouth parted at the sensation. "One where everyone wins, and then we go on with life the next day."

"Say the word and we won't play." Seth's thumb stroked the tender flesh on the inside of my arm.

Every inch of me ached for more. A kiss, a touch. Given how wet I was, if I shifted my weight, I'd slip and slide. Had they planned this? Did I care whether the moment was spontaneous? "Let's play."

Ryan pressed against me, and dipped his head. His teeth skittered along my throat and the hollow below. "I've been thinking, ever since Friday night." He dropped his fingers below the waistband of my jeans enough to tease, but didn't move lower. "How much I'd like to make that scene real. To fuck you hard and fast until you scream my name, while Seth watches, stroking his cock."

Oh geez. My knees wobbled, but the two of them were pressed close enough they'd hold me up if I stumbled. I didn't know which turned me on more. The thought of Ryan buried inside me, or the idea of being a private peep show for Seth.

"Still want to play?" Ryan's fingers skated over the top of my hip, and I thrust toward his touch before I realized what I was doing.

I managed a breathy, "Yes."

"You sure?" He gave me a wicked grin. "You're not just being polite? How do I know you mean it?"

My panties were practically soaked; that was a reasonable indicator. I worked a hand free from Seth's grip, and slid my fingers down the back of Ryan's arm, nudging it lower. "Check for yourself."

His hand moved down the front of my jeans, and I gasped when his fingers brushed my mound.

"You're so wet." He spread my pussy lips and dipped between. When he nudged my swollen clit, a shock of pleasure ripped through me. What if someone caught us? The idea heightened my arousal. We'd have to be careful.

With his free hand, he undid the button on my jeans and dragged down my zipper. He stroked my slit slowly, methodically, drawing near my aching sex, but not touching it again. I rocked my hips in time to the rhythm, pushing for more with each pass.

"So hot." Seth's breath caressed my skin. He let go of my other wrist, and slid his hands under my shirt. His rough palms against my bare stomach were another enticing point of contact. When he pushed one breast out of my bra, the sensation sparked across every inch of me. He tweaked my nipple and I pressed my ass back against him, grinding against his hard length. His groan mingled with mine when he rolled my pink nub between his fingers.

I found the bulge in Ryan's jeans, and he sucked in a sharp breath through his teeth when I stroked him through the rough fabric.

I inhaled sharply when he finally found my aching

clit again. I rocked between the two as Seth pinched hard, and Ryan caressed. Every time I rolled toward the edge of climax, Ryan eased off. I caught my bottom lip between my teeth, and fixed a desperate gaze on him. "Please?" The word came out breathlessly.

He gave me a wicked grin. "Please what?"

"I'm so close," I whimpered.

He caught my earlobe in his teeth, voice a low growl against my skin. "Beg me, Tash. Tell me what you want."

I couldn't say that. Not here. Even in the privacy of a house, I'd have a hard time with it. I shook my head.

"It's easy," he coaxed as he dragged his nose up the edge of my neck. His fingers dipped near my opening and then pulled away to tease my clit until my hips bucked, and he eased off again. "You don't have to scream. That can wait until we get home."

Oh gods, he had more in mind? The thought short-circuited my brain, and I pushed out the plea. "Please, Ryan. I'm so close. Let me come?"

He plunged his fingers inside me with a sudden thrust, and I had to bite the inside of my cheek to keep from crying out. His thumb found my clit, and he rubbed hard and fast, drawing tight circles. Orgasm rolled through me, and I ground against his hand when I came. My legs wobbled, but I had been right, the two of them kept me upright.

Ryan eased off down below as he pressed his forehead to mine. "We need privacy. Your place is closer."

I nodded, not sure I could speak.

"You ready to put on a show?"

"Oh, fuck yes." Seth's whisper echoed in my head, and he tugged me back into his stiff cock one more time before letting me go.

It took the last of my focus to fumble with my keys long enough to let us into my apartment. The moment we were inside, Ryan kicked the door shut and pinned me against it, arms over my head. "Now, I want to hear you scream."

I was going to argue the neighbors might not like that, but just then I didn't care. The entire ride home had been a series of exchanged teasing gropes. Me sliding my hand along Seth's inner thigh and stroking him through his jeans. Ryan reaching up from the back seat to cup my breasts.

Now that we were inside, Ryan held me in place, lowered his head to my neck, and sucked the sensitive flesh, biting hard occasionally and making my head swim. His voice was low but commanding when he finally let up. "See, Seth doesn't tell anyone this, but he's a voyeur." He let go of my wrists to yank my shirt over my head. I was certain something tore in the process, and positive I didn't care.

Heat and desire flooded me when two pairs of eyes raked over me.

Ryan continued. "But I don't think you're like that. I think you like the idea of being watched."

So much more than I'd ever realized before about an hour ago. "Maybe."

"Good." He followed my spine with a series of tantalizing taps until he reached my bra. More fluidly than I think even I was capable of, he twisted the clasps and snapped the lingerie open. He dragged the straps down my arms. I didn't think it was possible, but under his attention, my nipples got even harder. I heard a zipper drag down, and behind him I saw Seth drop into an easy chair, dick in hand, and slowly start to stroke. He really was well hung. What would it feel like to have that inside me?

Ryan trailed his lips down my collarbone and flicked a tongue over a hard pink nub. He grabbed my other breast, kneading one while he nibbled the other. The sensation was incredible, but I wanted more. I tugged the bottom of his shirt, and he broke away long enough for me to pull it over his head and toss it aside. He was so slender. I traced my fingers up his sides, marveling at every dip and nuance against my touch. When I dragged across one dark-brown nipple, he inhaled sharply and flicked his tongue fast and furious. I used my thumb to imitate his pace, and he moaned against my skin.

My other hand dropped to his crotch, and I found his erection again, stiff and eager through denim. I teased the bulge, and he jerked back with a grunt. He grabbed both of my wrists again. The rough gesture sent a spike of need through me.

Ryan pushed me toward the couch. "I'm so glad I bought condoms this morning."

Part of me wanted to read something into his comment, but I was focused on other things. When he spun me away from him, I caught Seth's gaze. He was still slowly stroking his cock, breathing heavily, and tiny smile played on his lips. Seeing that made me even wetter. I wanted him to get off watching us.

Ryan's front pressed into my back, and he made quick work of the button on my jeans. The zipper groaned open on its own when he yanked my bottoms to the ground, cotton and denim drawing friction as they were pushed aside.

He rested a hand on the middle of my back and pushed me forward. "Lean over the back of the couch."

I did as I was told, feeling more exposed than I ever had, and thrilled by every minute of it.

"I've always loved your ass." He gave it a light slap. "It looks even better bare."

The sting of his palm drew a new gasp from me.

"You like that?" He chuckled. He slapped one cheek again, harder this time. The pain was balanced by the pleasure of my pussy lips sliding together and vibrating around my engorged sex. He spanked me four or five more times.

As much as I enjoyed the new sensation, I wanted more. I forced the words out, loving the way they tasted rolling over my tongue. "I want you to fuck me."

His hand cupped a butt cheek and slid forward, fingers dipping in my wet, anxious opening. "I like the sound of that."

Me too. From behind, I heard his buckle clang, a zipper slide down, and the rip of foil. My anticipation spiked. My breath tore out in anxious, jagged pants. His fingers slid along my slit one more time, before the head of his cock nudged me.

He pushed inside with a single, hard thrust, and I cried out.

"Jesus." His words glided on my skin. "I'm not going to last long. You feel so good. So fucking tight."

I wanted to reply, but every time I managed to find the words, he slammed into my G-spot, slapping against my still tender behind with every grunt.

I was so close. I rode the edge of climax, head growing light and every sensation blurring into one another. When he found my clit again, it was like flipping a switch. "Oh, gods, Ryan, yes." I couldn't believe what was tearing from my throat, but it felt so intense. The orgasm flooded me, peaking again when his grunts reached my ears.

"I'm going to come, Tash. You're so tight. You fit perfectly on my cock." The words trailed off in a series of groans and frantic pounding. In the background, I was vaguely aware of Seth moaning, too.

Then everything slowed to as stop, and silence crashed in around us.

Ryan slipped out of me. He wrapped his hands around my waist and helped me stand. I wasn't sure my legs would support me, but he held me up. His cheek rested against my back, and his thumbs traced over my ribs. "Fuck, you're amazing."

I wanted to echo the sentiment, but I couldn't find the breath. I leaned into him, memorizing every lingering touch, and letting it meld with the bits of me that still stung pleasantly. "Ditto."

I WOKE UP THE NEXT MORNING TO A WARM BODY PRESSED against my back, and an arm draping over my stomach. I inhaled deeply, searing the memory of Seth's aftershave mixed with sex into my mind. Had last night really happened? After we'd all caught our breath, any remaining clothes came off, and I sucked Seth off while Ryan screwed me from behind again. Yeah, that had really happened. Wow.

Seth's hand glided up my stomach and brushed the bottom of my breast. "Morning, Tasha."

"Mmm..." I arched my back at the teasing contact, and need throbbed between my legs. I wasn't going to dwell on if this was awkward or not. We'd agreed last night it was just fun and games. A pang echoed inside at the idea this wouldn't happen again, and I pushed it away. I couldn't get attached to them, partly because I'd never be able to choose, but mostly because I wasn't going to scare either guy off by being *that girl* who didn't know the difference between sex and love.

That didn't mean I was in a rush to extract myself from Seth's arms. Or that I could ignore the hard length pressed into my back, and how wet I was getting as he drew closer to my nipple, but never quite touched the rigid nub.

"We have an eight a.m." Disappointment tempered his tone. "Otherwise, there are so many things I'd like to do to you. Hell, I'm tempted anyway."

Damn it. Why did work have to be so…consistent? I wiggled my ass against his erection as one final tease and reminder and then reluctantly rolled away. "I guess you're right."

As I climbed out of bed, he grabbed my wrist and pulled me back to my knees on the mattress. He sat up in front of me, and rested a hand at the back of my neck, light eyes locked on mine. "Even though it was *just a game*, I had an incredible time last night."

Did he sound disappointed the night before hadn't meant anything? Before I could question the hesitation in his statement, he pressed his lips to mine. The soft kiss seeped into my senses, searing my thoughts. I leaned into him with a groan. Electricity danced along my skin when his tongue dove into my mouth.

His dick dug into my bare stomach, tempting me. I trailed my fingers along his chest, seconds away from moving my hands lower. He held my head captive and deepened the kiss, crushing my lips into my teeth.

Every inch of me was on fire with need. We could miss our meeting, right? I nipped at his bottom lip, and let my palm slide down.

He broke away with a gasp, stopping me before I could wrap my fingers around his cock. His hooded gaze swept over me, his voice an octave lower than normal. "So, so tempting."

I'd have to settle for that. It was still a fantastic way to end a fantastic fling. I caught my bottom lip between my teeth. "Had to try."

Something occurred to me, and I strained my ears for a second, listening for any other sounds in the small apartment. Nope, nothing. "Where's Ryan?"

Seth's shoulders slumped. "Early meeting. He had to jet."

"Oh." I needed to keep the disappointment from my voice. It's not as if I could expect him to wake me up. Hell, I was lucky Seth had stuck around. I shifted my weight and the slickness between my legs was obvious. I was *really* lucky Seth had stuck around.

"Yeah." He scrambled to his feet.

With the morning light peeking through the blinds, I got to see what had been shadowed the night before. He really was gorgeous. Just the right amount of muscle tone, handsome face, and—my gaze paused on his crotch—as well hung as his roommate. The thought flushed my skin.

I really needed to get ready for work, and if I asked him to join me in the shower, I was sure that would cross a line, and make us both late. "Do you need me to drop you off at home?"

"Sure." His enthusiasm sounded forced.

Had I missed something?

Would things be different with Ryan this morning? Conversation with Seth had felt forced in the car, but he assured me several times we were fine. By the time I dropped him off, he'd relaxed enough I believed him. Would I have to go through the same ritual with Ryan? He wasn't at his desk when I got in, and a trickle of disappointment joined my paranoia.

I forced myself to sit and finish prepping for our meeting. It was another client call, this one with the entire team. I'd sent my updated timeline to Mark yesterday afternoon, and even though he hadn't signed off, he would.

"Hey, Tash." Ryan tugged a few loose strands of my hair, and relief rushed a smile onto my face. "Sleep well last night?"

Pink flooded my cheeks. "Better than in a long time."

"Glad to hear it. " He moved back to his own cube and dropped into his seat.

That seemed to go okay. Nothing to worry about, we were all still friends. Except I knew my fantasies were going to be vivid and rampant and involving one or the other or both of them for a long time. But that was only barely different from before, right?

Seth walked in with just minutes to spare before the meeting, and gave us both a weak smile as we all took our seats in the conference room. I was surprised to see Mark already there, his laptop hooked up to the online meeting and projector. Normally that would be my job. Worry leaked into my thoughts.

No big deal. He was just making sure Zedophap knew we were serious about fixing the situation; that was all. And he had another business analyst in the room because he'd recruited someone else to help us with the work. That had to be it. I repeated the reassurance enough times I almost believed it.

After brief introductions on both sides—that wouldn't have been necessary except they had members of their upper management on the phone, never a good sign—we launched into the call. As the formalities and basic repetition dragged on, I remembered just how little sleep I'd gotten the night before.

When Mark pulled up the adjusted timeline, my gut sank further. It wasn't the one I'd presented to him. It was far more aggressive, and completely implausible. I literally bit my tongue to keep from calling him on it in front of the client, but I was already composing my response in my head for when I could speak to him off the record.

"What about the configuration problems? How do we know those won't happen in the future?" That was one of Zedophap's VP's.

"Our project manager has tracked down the problem. I can assure you Ryan Coleman is being pulled from the project and someone new who's been brought up to speed on the sensitive nature of this project will be taking his spot for the duration."

My head shot up, eyes wide, and my gaze locked on Ryan's across the room. His jaw clenched and he gave an almost imperceptible shake of his head before he looked away. Bile rose in my throat. Fuck, that wasn't how this was supposed to go. My right eye twitched, and I rubbed my temples to try and stave off a headache.

Ryan was the first out the door when the call was over, and I hurried after him. "Ryan, wait, please?"

He kept walking, brushing past a couple of pockets of our coworkers, and not pausing until we were in the empty break room. He whirled on me, eyes narrowed. His voice was low enough only I would hear it. "What the fuck was that?"

"I don't—"

"No." He held up his index finger. "You threw me under the bus."

"I didn't." This wasn't right. It didn't mesh with what Mark told me yesterday. None of it clicked. I really had sold him out and I hadn't even realized it. "I'm sorry. This wasn't supposed to happen."

"You know what? I don't care." His angry tone wavered. "Just don't talk to me right now, okay?"

He brushed past me without making physical or eye contact. I just needed to let him cool down. This would pass, and then I could apologize. Except no matter how many times I tried to tell myself that, there was a part of me whispering about how devastated I would be if he didn't forgive me.

He already had his head down, typing furiously, when I got back to my desk. He didn't even glance in my direction. I needed to talk to Mark, but his door was closed. And the voicemail light on my phone was blinking. The caller ID said it was my landlord.

Please let just this one thing go right for me. I dialed up the message.

"I'm so sorry, hon, but I can't afford to keep having this happen. I have bills I need to pay, too. Your deposit will cover the rest of the rent for the month, but I need you out after that."

I was being evicted? Nausea rolled through me as I hung up the phone. I was going to be ill.

My messenger chimed, with a note from Seth. *You couldn't have at least given him a heads-up he was about to be crucified?*

Oh gods.

The email from Mark in my inbox should have made me feel better. I think it was meant to. *Sorry I couldn't warn you, but you did great. We've don't have a choice on the updated timeline, but I know you can make it work.*

But the email from Ryan in my personal inbox was worse. It wasn't addressed to me; it had gone to our entire AD&D circle. It just said, *Can't make Friday's game. Maybe not again. Find another venue. I hope this is enough warning.*

I dropped my head in my hands, trying to keep my fractured thoughts from pulling my skull apart and spilling out my forehead. Tears stung my eyes and every inch of me ached with frustration. I couldn't do this. I didn't know how I was going to make any of this right, let alone all of it.

I worked through lunch, telling myself it was because I had so much to do and didn't want the peanut butter and jelly sandwich I'd brought. Really, I couldn't have stomached food even if I had time.

Neither Seth nor Ryan talked to me the rest of the day. I tried to initiate conversations when I passed by, but I never got more than a grunt in response. I wanted to believe they were being babies about this, but given how heavy the threat had been for me to make the project right again, they were probably under similar pressure.

I spent that night scouring the Internet and want ads for cheap apartments. My current one bedroom had been a fantastic deal, and I'd be lucky to find a cramped studio basement for the same price. Especially since I couldn't pass a credit check, and I'd be breaking my wallet to afford any deposit at all. There was no way I could manage something like first and last month's rent.

The next day at work was a repeat of the previous, with Ryan even turning and walking out of the break room in the middle of me saying hello.

I spent half the workday staring at my monitor. I needed to be doing something. Working, figuring out the housing problem, something. But every time I tried to redirect my thoughts, they drifted back to how to get Ryan to forgive me. Or at least, how to set things right for him. Even if I'd screwed things up so bad he never spoke to me again—an idea that gnawed me from the inside out—I'd never forgive myself if I'd done something like destroy his career.

My cell phone vibrated against my desk, jerking me from my rambling panic. My landlord. At least for the next couple of weeks. Dread made every inch of me feel like I was made of lead as I extracted myself from my chair. I didn't know if I had the strength for whatever this was about but ignoring it would only make things worse, if only because it would send my stress sensors into overload.

"Hello," I was already talking as I locked my computer and strolled to a more private part of the building to take the call.

We made small talk for a few moments. Her polite attitude and the underlying apology in her voice made some of my tension evaporate. "I'm sorry to bother you at work, hon," she said. "And I hate to ask this. I haven't put your place on the market yet, but some friends of the family are looking, and they're interested in your apartment. Is there any chance I can bring them by in the next couple of days? Feel free to say no, of course. It's still your place."

For now. My shoulders slumped and I rubbed my temples. I needed to start packing anyway. This sounded like an extra dash of motivation. "Sure. Anytime this weekend." Especially if our AD&D game was off, maybe forever. "Just give me a little warning first."

We said our goodbyes and I slunk back to my chair. I didn't like these feelings of impotence and frustration. I was used to being in control. To having a solution. But now? I couldn't see anything past the fog of negativity in my brain.

I dropped in to my chair with a soft, "Oof." Irresolution clawed at my throat, and stung my eyes with unshed tears. I would not break down in the middle of the office. That would be one misstep too many.

I breathed deep through my nose to try and calm myself. There were answers. I just needed to stop wallowing and spinning my wheels and find them. First things first. I didn't want to be homeless at the end of the month.

Opening a web browser, I typed in *cheap cash only housing*. I didn't think it would get me anywhere, but nothing else had either, so I needed to try a new approach. My eyes grew wide at one of the paid search results that popped up. I knew the image, and the logo. I drove by the motel every night on my way home from work.

But that was just it. It was a motel. I needed something long term. I clicked the link anyway, mind whirring to catch up with solutions I couldn't quite grasp. As I scanned their page—weekly rates, discounts for storage, small cash deposit—hope crept in.

It was a little more expensive than what I was paying now, but considering the cost included utilities, cable, and internet… It would give me a place to crash until I could save a little more money.

I felt better than I had all week. I still needed to figure out what to do about Ryan and Seth. But now I could focus exclusively on them.

ON THURSDAY, MY GUT SANK WHEN RYAN'S DESK WAS empty. The clock ticked past nine, and then ten, and he still didn't show up. Had I really cost him his job? The possibility made me want to retch.

I shouldn't think like that. His own inability to take the project seriously had done this. Still, I could have given him more warning. Tried harder to make it right. And something told me I didn't have all the facts. Too bad he wasn't giving them to me.

By the time lunch rolled around, I was too ill with imagined scenarios to have any interest in the sandwich I hadn't touched on Tuesday or Wednesday, either. I needed answers. Since Ryan was ignoring my texts, I'd have to go to a different source.

I said a brief prayer Seth wouldn't make me raise my voice to have this conversation, and stepped into his cubicle. I fumbled for words I probably should have composed before I got there.

He looked up from his computer, brows raised. "So we're finally going to stop this?"

"I— Yes?" I should feel relieved, but the lack of anything but irritation in his voice set my nerves further on edge.

"Good." He grabbed his sunglasses and kept his voice low. "Get your purse, we'll go to lunch, and you can tell me why you're not eating, why you're looking for a new apartment, and…" He glanced around, gaze pausing on Mark's open office door. "Other things."

I wasn't going to tell him about the first two. No way in hell. And the twenty-two cents in my bank account wasn't going to let me eat out. But I did want to have the "other things" conversation. "I was thinking we could just go outside for a little bit. Enjoy the sun. Chat. You know."

He sighed as he stood. His hand at the small of my back summoned wants I shouldn't have, but I couldn't bring myself to pull away. He reached over the top of my cubicle, grabbed my purse, and handed it to me. "Lunch is on me. No arguments."

We made our way outside, and I dropped into his passenger seat when he held the door open for me. I twisted my fingers in and out of each other, trying to compose my story. He'd ask me again about skipping lunches, I knew he wouldn't drop it that easily, but I could skate over the details. Tell him it was nothing and I had it under control. Then we could talk about Ryan.

A knot formed in my chest when he pulled into the parking lot of my favorite pub. They had the best steak sandwiches anywhere, and I was suddenly painfully aware of how little I'd eaten over the past few days. He still didn't push for any information as we were seated. We both had our regular lunches, but I couldn't ask him to spend that kind of money. I scanned the menu for something inexpensive.

When the waitress arrived, he placed his order and I asked for a large bowl of the soup of the day.

"No." Seth cut me off before I could finish. "She'll have the rib eye on sourdough, onion rings, not fries, and a diet Coke. And we need another of those sandwiches to go."

Embarrassment raced through me. Great, now I felt like a starving orphan or something. I couldn't look at him.

"Hey." The irritation was gone from his voice. Under the table, he nudged my shoe with his. "Tell me what's up, please?"

"I'm fine." The lie was harder to force out than it should be. Suddenly, every inch of me desperately wanted to spill my guts. But I couldn't unburden myself to him. "A little short on cash until payday. Nothing big. It happens."

His lips drew into a thin line. "You've been drinking work coffee—which I know you hate—instead of bringing your own from home. Your lunch bag has sat untouched on your desk for three days, and you hide a long string of apartment listings anytime someone walks by your desk. Tell me, please?"

His expression was so sincere, the edges of his blue eyes soft with concern. Something inside gave under the uncertainty and tension, and I spilled everything about my money problems. Being broke, being evicted, ignoring calls from creditors who weren't mine, and dealing with judgments. It felt good to finally have shared, but it still didn't jar any solutions loose.

Wrinkles creased his brow. "You should have told us. We could have helped. You could probably borrow money from Ryan."

Just the mention of that was enough to make me ill all over again. "No. Nuh-uh. I can't."

"Why not?"

"First of all, I can't do that to our friendship. Even borrowing fifty bucks would hang over my head, and I'm so much further behind than that. Second, he hates me. Third, he's not even here today. He didn't get fired, did he?"

Seth let out a slow breath. "No, he didn't get fired. He just decided he could take a day off since his schedule has cleared up recently. He called in sick." He made air quotes around the word *sick*.

Relief coursed through me. At least he wasn't unemployed.

But Seth wasn't done. "Speaking of, though. He doesn't hate you, but the fact you completely screwed him over is going to hang over your head a lot more than asking for a couple hundred bucks that I can almost guarantee he'd never want you to pay back."

"I didn't know that he was going to be fed to the Zedophap dogs like that." All the rationalizations I'd told myself over the past few days rushed back, but they sounded weak now. Still, I pushed them out. "I tried to ask him about the issues, and he brushed me off. You were there." Even to my own ears, I sounded more as if I was trying to convince myself than him.

"Three years ago, Ryan slept with Kitner's wife at the company Christmas party."

Whatever I had expected Seth to say, Ryan getting it on with the boss's wife was nowhere on the list. If I'd counted out to one hundred, it might have landed somewhere around a serious, *We're KGB sleeper agents, and now I have to kill you because you know.* Jealousy surged inside with the news, and I wasn't sure how to react. "He never told me that."

Seth raised an eyebrow. "You never told him your ex-husband bankrupted you."

Touché. "But… I mean… I know he screws around, but an affair?"

"To be fair, she told him she was the new girl in accounting. He had no idea she was even married until he saw them arguing at the end of the party.

And Kitner's marriage was already on the rocks. That was just one of many catalysts."

The story hit me hard, not because of the nature of it, though that was heavy too, but because it pointed out how little I knew about both of them. And I wanted to know more. Not just best friend stuff, but everything. "I didn't realize."

"I know. You also probably had no idea Kitner is screwing your new business analyst. The one who took Ryan's place on the Zedophap account."

Shit. The pieces started to slide into place. Mark wanted a new job for his girlfriend; he made things up to make it happen. Except… "The config really was wrong. And I tried to ask Ryan about it and he brushed me off."

Seth shrugged. "I wish you'd trusted him. I don't know what happened, but he didn't screw this up. You know that, right?"

Part of me did, and that was a large bit of what had me feeling so horrible. I'd let stress override common sense and friendship. "I have to apologize. You have to tell him to hear me out. Please?"

"I will. Anything you want." His smile had a trace of sadness I didn't understand. "Follow me home after work, and I'll sit on him if I have to."

The imagery made me giggle, and it released a load of tension, making my chest lighter. Nothing was solved, but life didn't seem hopeless anymore. Even if Ryan forgave me, I still wasn't asking to borrow money, but one step at a time.

9

I managed to make it through the rest of the workday on fifty percent concentration. I kept coming up with new variations on how I'd apologize to Ryan. Would he even hear me out?

And my mind kept drifting back to lunch. Why did something feel different talking to Seth? There was an odd kind of comfort, but at the same time a sadness I'd never felt from him before. I had to be projecting. Letting stress get to me. But I couldn't get past the idea I was still missing so many pieces, both with him, and with the project at work.

That evening, I parked my car next to the curb in front of their house as Seth took his spot in the driveway. The nervous apprehension I'd been trying to fight all day surged forward with a vengeance as I followed him up the walk to the front door. When we pushed inside, Ryan was on the couch, Xbox controller in hand, entire body ducking and weaving with whatever he was playing. He looked up when the door creaked, and his grin faded when his eyes met mine.

He tossed the controller on the couch and stood. "I'll be in my room."

Seth stepped forward, but I pulled him back. This was my mistake. "Wait, please." I tried to keep my voice firm, but a waver snuck in.

"What, Natasha?" At his use of my full name, something cracked in my chest. "You didn't listen to me, why should I do any differently for you?"

My carefully crafted apology evaporated, and the words spilled out before I could consider them. "I'm so, so sorry. I didn't know. Based on what I saw, what was I supposed to think? And I shouldn't have done it anyway, you deserve better than that. I just didn't know what else to do. And I—"

"Stop." The single word snapped through the room. "I can't. You never realize. It doesn't matter how obvious it is. How in your face it is, you don't get it."

Something told me we weren't just talking about work anymore.

Seth stepped around me, crossing the room with rapid strides, and stopping nose to nose with Ryan. His voice was the same low, controlled tone he'd used earlier today, but with an angry roar lining it. "Don't yell at her. She made a mistake, and she's apologizing for it. But you… This last week has been a game for you. You've even said so. Your exact words. You're using her affection for you. She's wanted you since she met you, and it's just a tumble to you."

My words stuck in my throat. How did he know that? I always thought I'd hidden it so well. I should be humiliated that the truth was coming out now, but it felt good. I wanted Ryan to know. I just wished it was under different circumstances, and that it didn't mean pushing Seth away in the process. Gods, please don't let me lose Seth over this.

Ryan's voice was low, but it carried through the entire room. There was no mistaking the threat in each emphasized word. "Walk away now."

"Fuck you." Seth's calm vanished with his reply. "You don't give a shit about her, not like I do. You don't even care about me the way I do you. Now that this is all over, and you got off, you'll move on."

My brain hitched and stumbled over the words, and despite my trepidation, warmth spread inside at the realization. Had he just said…? He had. Seth cared about me. About Ryan. How had I not seen that? "I—"

Ryan held up a hand, never looking at me, but it was enough to silence me. He rested both palms on Seth's cheeks and kissed him hard. One of them moaned—or maybe it was both of them. I expected to feel a pang of jealousy, but instead pure liquid heat filled my veins. Gods, that was hot. I wanted to be a part of the desire flowing between them as Seth traced the visible bulge of the erection straining against Ryan's jeans.

Ryan finally broke the kiss. The anger in his tone had been replaced with breathlessness. "You're wrong. I love you both so hard, and I don't know what I'd do without either one of you."

Love. The word bounced in my skull, feeling both terrifying and right at the same time. How had I never seen that? "I had no idea." I clamped my jaw shut when two heads swiveled in my direction, and I realized I'd spoken out loud.

Ryan moved to stand in front of me, and nudged a curl off my forehead. "No kidding." He nodded over his shoulder in Seth's direction. "He wasn't supposed to push this, either. We both agreed we wouldn't pressure you. That if you made up your mind somewhere along the way, we were fine with it. But seriously, Tash. I'm tired of dancing around this." He nipped my lower lip, and my chest almost burst. "I don't want you to pick. I want you, and I want him. I'm selfish."

The blood had rushed from my head, leaving me a little stupid, and incredibly turned on. "But you're not…"

"Gay?" His mouth twisted in amusement, and he trailed a finger along the edge of my ear. "Nope. But you have to admit, Seth's hot."

"I'm not going to argue with that."

"It took the two of you long enough," Seth teased.

Ryan laughed, his attention still on me. "I've been thinking about it for a while, and Friday night kind of pushed me over the edge. Monday cemented it for me. But you still didn't get it. I had to walk away. Get some distance from you. Figure out what I was going to do if you really weren't interested."

So that was why he hadn't been talking to me? "I'm so interested. I thought you were mad about work."

"I am. I'm furious." His roaming hand fisted in my hair, and he yanked. "But I also get it. And we'll deal with it."

His kiss was as incredible as Seth's had been the other morning, but in a very different direction. Instead of safety and security, this was heat, and want, and everything nasty I tried to pretend I didn't dream about. Rough sex and handprints on my ass and sleepless nights I'd do again and again if I had the chance. He tugged my hair back, and his teeth lightly scraped along my throat. He bit into the fleshy, sensitive part of my neck, and sucked until I swore I might come just from the hickey. I shifted against him, and the friction built.

He finally pulled back, holding my head captive and looking me in the eye. "Mine."

I had never wanted to be possessed before, and now it felt right. "Yours," I repeated.

He grabbed my fingertips and tugged me toward the back of the house, where the bedrooms were. My pulse seared with flames under my skin, making my nipples ache against their prison. Damp need grew between my legs.

He sat on the edge of his bed and then let go of my

hand. Confusion flitted in as he stared up at me with expectation.

"Take off your clothes," Seth commanded from behind me. "Slow. A piece at a time. Every eye in the room is on you."

Gods, the two of them were going to kill me, and I was going to die happy.

10

Bold mischievousness coursed through me, and I stepped out of Ryan's reach. A glance over my shoulder told me Seth was near the doorway. I pushed a hint of teasing into my voice. "If I'm putting on a show, then that's all it is. No touching."

Ryan smirked. "We'll see."

My fingers glided down the front of my shirt, undoing each button along the way, but not pulling the sides apart. The two pairs of eyes on me lit my every nerve ending on fire. I moved to my skirt next, undoing it and letting it fall to the floor. Stepping out of it, I kicked that and my heels aside.

I stood in the middle of the room, shirt barely covering my panty-clad ass and hinting at what lay underneath in front. My pussy ached for attention, and my breasts strained against fabric, begging to be touched. Ryan's hand drifted to his crotch, rubbing lightly through denim as his hungry eyes traced over my body.

Seth moaned, and I wondered if he was doing the same. I was too lost in my light striptease to look. I let my shirt slide to the ground, and moved my palms to my bra. I cupped each mound through the lace, squeezing enough to draw out my own sigh, but not sating the desire. I wanted more.

My fingers trailed down my stomach, past the top of my panties, and to my wet mound. I slid the crotch aside enough to give a peek and stroked my slit lightly. My eyes closed at my own touch. It still wasn't what I wanted, but knowing the impact it was having on both men made me lightheaded.

I was so lost in the moment, my heart jumped when Seth grabbed me from behind. "Another day." His voice was low. I leaned back, and his bare skin met mine. When had his clothes come off? I wanted to spin and take him in, but he held me captive. He shoved up the bottom of my bra, and the rough elastic bit into my skin.

I whimpered for more and he obliged, lips tracing light lines along the back of my neck while he caressed my skin. He kissed along my ear. "Don't get me wrong, I like watching." He trailed his tongue over my skin. "But sometimes, I want to participate. I need to know what it feels like to be inside you."

"Me too."

He stripped off the remainder of my clothes and moved in front of me. Ryan stood, putting him only a few inches from Seth. The two stared each other down, and the seconds ticked away. Ryan's hand glided down Seth's chest and wrapped around his sheathed cock. He kissed Seth hard, a hungry snarl rising between them, and pulled back again just as abruptly.

"Be good to her," Ryan warned.

Seth gave a light laugh and shoved him aside. "Trust me, the rough stuff is more fun to watch. It's all yours."

Ryan gave me a wicked wink and slid out of sight.

Seth sat near the edge of the bed, dick at attention, and pulled me toward him. "I want to watch you ride me."

I licked my lips and straddled him. I wrapped my hand around his cock, and he closed his eyes with a sigh. I slid the thick head along my slit, before slowly impaling myself. "Gods, you're so big," I moaned.

I rocked slowly against him, our breathing shifting until we were in perfect sync. His hands roamed up my chest, softly cupping my tits, and his gaze never stopped roaming my body. Every time I tried to increase the pace, he'd slow me back down. One hand dropped, and his thumb brushed my aching sex.

"Please?" I begged.

He smiled. "I'm not him. You can't beg me for hard and fast." He trailed circles around the swollen nub, exposing it and stroking it at the same rhythmic pace he glided in and out of me.

He shifted his attention, and rubbed my clit

harder. An abrupt spark raced through me, stealing the air from my head, and I plummeted over an edge I hadn't known I was on. I clenched around his cock as I came, panting and grinding against his hand.

A pair of fingers slipped between my legs from behind, trailing through my juices and drawing the slick wet back. I gasped with a new kind of pleasure when Ryan's finger glided along my asshole.

"You like that?" Hand on my back he pushed me forward.

Seth guided me down until my chest was pressed against his, still rocking inside me.

Ryan's fingers glided along my slit again, and this time one slipped into my ass without a problem. "I'll be gentle this time." His seductive tone rolled off my skin. "Just relax."

Something nudged my back door, and I moaned at the push.

"Tell me if you want me to stop."

"Gods, no." There was pain, but he eased in slowly, and being stretched out from both sides felt amazing.

Ryan laughed. "I so completely adore you." His hands gripped my hips, and both men resumed rocking, one slamming into me from behind, and the other driving deep into my pussy.

Seth took one nipple into his mouth, and sucked hard. Ryan's fingers dug into my pelvis hard. Would he leave bruises? I hoped so. The multiple points of contact penetrated every one of my senses. I was so close to coming again. I lost track of the specific sensations. I was moaning both their names, sinking into lightheaded ecstasy as they fucked me at the same time. This time climax crept up slowly, washing over me in waves that mingled with everything else.

Seth grunted and his attentions to my breast paused. He threw his head back with a groan, pushing hard and fast until he was spent inside me. I recognized similar sounds from behind. Moments later Ryan slipped out with a quiet, "Fuck, Tash. Just… Fuck."

I giggled at the sudden release of tension in the room, and buried my face in Seth's muscular chest. My words were muffled. "I love you both. You should know that. Intensely and deeply, and I can't believe I was so dim."

Seth lifted my head enough to press his lips to my forehead. "Not dim. You just need to learn to trust yourself."

Seconds later, Ryan dropped onto the mattress next to us, tugging me back into him. He kissed my shoulder blades. For the first time since I could remember, he didn't say anything. He just held me.

11

Thank the gods it was Friday. Finally. This had been the longest week of my life. A smile played on my face as I rolled onto my back and found Ryan's bedroom ceiling above me instead of my own. And I would do it again in a heartbeat. I'd take the bad with the good, if it turned out like this. The sound of the shower running provided background noise to my contentment. Last night had been amazing.

I wasn't even concerned about my looming eviction. I had the inklings of a plan. It wasn't much, but it was a start.

A warm weight rested on my legs—the familiar sensation of flesh against flesh teasing me—and seconds later Ryan's face appeared over mine. He pinned my hands above my head, and traced his lips along my neck. His words vibrated against the sensitive skin when he spoke. "You're going to be late for work, sexy."

Right, I couldn't lay here all day. And I should probably tell him to un-cancel the AD&D game before tonight. Something popped into my head without permission, and I realized what it felt like to have the light bulb go off. "How long has Mark been screwing around?"

Ryan pulled back enough for me to see his frown. "I'm going to draw a line right there. It's not a turn on to talk about any kind of sex from the guy who wants my job so bad he probably beats off to the fantasy."

I reluctantly nudged him off me, disappointment rushing in to take the place of his body pressed against mine. I sat up, latched onto my growing idea. "I'm serious. How long?"

"I don't know. A couple of months. Seth said they were having problems, but I guess he read them wrong."

Oh motherfucker. I really was dim. "And you swear to me you filled that config doc out exactly the way the client said?"

His mouth twisted in disbelief, and his brows rose. "I'm pretending you didn't ask that."

I rolled forward on my knees, and brushed my lips over his. "I need to go home and get dressed. I'll see you in the office."

He tangled his fingers in my curls and pulled me in, deepening the kiss. When we broke apart, I struggled to find my breath. I hoped I never got used to that rush. I gave him a shy smile and scooted to the edge of the bed. I plucked my shirt from the floor, and frowned when I realized last night's activities had covered the silk in something that was probably sticky once upon a time, and was now just kind of hard.

He nipped my earlobe. "Sorry about that." He didn't sound the least bit sorry. Seconds later, he was holding something over my shoulder. "Wear this."

I tugged his T-shirt over my head, inhaling deeply at the faint traces of his cologne mixed with laundry soap. "If you insist. And seriously, I need to go."

He laid a tender line of kisses along the back of my neck. "I guess."

I reluctantly pulled away, picking up the pace when I saw how late it was. I was in such a rush to make it to the front door, I collided with Seth when he emerged from the bathroom in nothing but a pair of boxers. I smacked into him, palms resting against his firm chest. "Sorry."

"Don't worry about it." He kissed me. His erection dug into my leg, making me regret even more we all had places to be. He stepped behind me and gave my ass a light smack, pushing me toward the front door. "Go."

THERE WAS A CUP OF COFFEE WAITING FOR ME ON MY desk when I got to work. TASHA written on the sleeve in familiar block letters, and what I think was a goblin to the right of it. Both my guys were already at their desks, heads down and working. *My guys*—I adored the sound of that. I dropped into my chair and dove into work.

Almost three hours later, I had a stack of log files, and all the proof I'd been hoping to find.

My messenger pinged with a note from Seth. *Lunch? No money isn't an excuse.*

We'd still have to talk about that. As much as I liked the idea of letting my boyfriends spoil me—and loved the plural—I wasn't going to be the leech my ex had been. But for today, I'd let it slide. Besides, with any luck I'd have news in exchange for the meal by the time noon rolled around. I sent back a quick, *I won't argue, just this once,* and then locked my computer and made my way to Mark's office.

He looked up when I knocked. "Natasha, come on in."

My nerves bunched in on themselves, and I hesitated. No, I needed to do this. I closed the door behind me. His brows rose as I took a seat and set my stack of papers face down on the desk. "We need to talk about Zedophap."

His back went rigid, and his jaw clenched for a moment. His casual, "Sure," defied every tense inch of his posture. "But I have a meeting in five, so it'll have to be fast."

"I'm sure we can cover what we need." I hoped I sounded more confident than I felt. This might all still blow up in my face. It could cost me a job I couldn't afford to lose, which would obliterate my half-formed plan to not be homeless. But I also needed to do this. Letting it slide wasn't right.

"Great, so what can I do for you?"

I flipped the documents over, and slid the first one across his desk. "This is the log from the configuration interface, showing that on Sunday afternoon, someone with administrative rights logged into the system and changed almost everything associated with Zedophap."

I pushed the next page to him. "This is from the source control software, showing that early Monday morning, someone replaced all of the documentation from the then business analyst with something entirely different."

I slid the next print out toward him. "This—"

He rested his hand on the papers. "Where are you going with this?"

My hands shook, and my heart was threatening to tear from my ribcage, I was so nervous. I pushed the words out. "This tells me Ryan isn't responsible for the screw up earlier this week. But someone with your login might have been. Possibly someone you're close to. Someone you're sleeping with?"

"There aren't any company rules against fraternization."

Thank the gods for that. I was feeling both more confident and more terrified as the conversation progressed. "No. But I don't think upper management would be too thrilled with your girlfriend sabotaging a major client to worm herself into a better position."

"Where's this going?" An edge crept into his voice. "Blackmail? Extortion? None of that's going to fly."

I hadn't even considered something like blackmail. The guys were right, I was a little dim. But I was fine with it in this case. I didn't want to be *that* person. "Gods, no. I was just thinking you'd tear up Ryan's write-up, you'd apologize to him for the mistake—you don't even have to do it publicly—and then we make sure this doesn't happen again."

Mark's eyes narrowed. "You don't think big, Natasha. That's always been your problem, and I suspect it always will be. This creates a rift you don't want in your career."

"I can handle it. I've seen what it's like to be on your shit list." I nodded at the paperwork. "And I know how to cover my ass if it happens again to me or anyone assigned to any of my projects."

His lip pulled into a sneer. "I have a meeting. You've made your point."

"Have I?" I didn't want to push him too far, but I had to be sure this wasn't just lip service.

"Yes." His bark filled the room. His tone returned to normal when he said, "we're done here."

Sick giddiness flowed through me as I sat back at my desk again. Things wouldn't drop as easily as it seemed like they just had, but I'd meant what I said about being able to cover my own ass.

There was a text from Ryan waiting for me when I got back to my desk. *Game's back on tonight. You know Ardra missed me.*

Why hadn't he emailed the group? My stomach fluttered at the teasing. He was just a few desks away, but this was low-key and playful, and not something I wanted anyone overhearing. Well, except one person. I sent back a response, and added Seth to the thread. *Galahad set her expectations high. Sure he can keep it up?*

A soft snorting laugh filtered through the cubicles, and seconds later, I had another text. *I'm having a hard time doing anything but keeping it up, and that's just from thinking about your bare ass.*

Heat flooded my cheeks, and I squirmed in my seat. Maybe work wasn't the best place for this. *We're talking about the game.*

Bullshit we are.

A giggle slipped past my lips, and I winced and clamped my mouth shut.

A new message from Seth interrupted the banter. *Some of us are trying to work.*

I raised my eyebrows at my phone. Was he really pissed off?

Seconds later, he followed it with, *Unless there are pictures. I'll drop everything for pictures.*

Goodie. Bossman wants to talk to me. Ryan's message killed my cheer in instant. I wanted to send him a quick *good luck,* but he was already walking away from his desk.

Please, please don't let me have made things worse. I swore the fifteen minutes from the time Kitner's door closed behind Ryan, until it re-opened, were the longest of my life. I'd taken a risk with what I'd done, but the full impact didn't hit me until I was stuck here waiting, without answers.

When Ryan re-emerged, he didn't look at anyone. He cut a straight line to his desk and seconds later, disappeared into the hallway leading to the back stairs.

A few moments later, my phone buzzed with a new text, and I thought my heart was going to explode out of my chest from the tension. It was from Ryan, and just said, *Take a break and meet me by the tree?*

Sure.

I tried to keep my pulse from tearing out of my veins, and my pace even and slow, as I followed a similar path to his. There was a tree with a bench near the office. We ate lunch there sometimes when the weather was good. And now I couldn't believe it was almost a five-minute walk. My nervousness was cranked up another notch by the fact I could see Ryan pacing long before I got to him.

As I drew closer, he crossed the last several yards between us, tangled his fingers in my hair, and kissed me hard.

I groaned and molded against him. I hadn't expected that, but I wasn't complaining.

When he broke away, he rested his forehead against mine. "It was a really stupid thing to do."

Shit. Had he been fired after all? I hadn't been bluffing with Kitner, I would make the information I had public, but I hadn't expected to have to. "I didn't—"

He cut me off with another brief kiss, nipping my bottom lip before he pulled away. "You're going to have to tell me what you said to him, because he was practically spitting venom when your name came up. But whatever it was, it worked. He destroyed my write-up."

I exhaled in relief. "You scared me."

He pushed a loose curl off my forehead. "Serves you right. Fill me in next time. Fill me in this time. And you know your life just got miserable at work, right?"

I nodded, agreeing to all three requests at once. "It was worth it. What he did was bullshit. And it'll cost him his job eventually."

He wrapped his arms around my waist, and I rested my cheek against his chest. His words vibrated through my ear when he spoke. "Just make sure it doesn't cost you yours first."

"That's the plan."

He traced tiny circles along the small of my back. "Good. Text Seth. Tell him early lunch. And you can give us all the juicy details."

I smiled, though he couldn't see me. "Yes, sir."

WHEN I PULLED UP IN FRONT OF RYAN AND SETH'S place, I thought it was odd there wasn't a single other car there yet. I was never the last one to arrive, but a couple of our players were consistently early. Maybe it had been too short a notice for everyone to show. Which was a little disappointing, but it would mean fewer people had to leave before we had the house to ourselves.

That made me pause. Were we telling anyone about our relationship? Even more important, why had we un-canceled game night when we had an entire weekend to explore this incredible new thing between us?

Well, maybe not the entire weekend. I still needed to pack up most of my stuff, move it into storage, and figure out how little I could get away with keeping on me and still be comfortable in my motel room. But that could wait at least a little while.

The door swung open before I could knock, and Seth stood on the other side.

I gave an exaggerated glance around me, pretending to look for someone else. "Expecting someone?"

He stepped in, rested a hand on the small of my back, and his mouth crushed down on mine. I intertwined my fingers at the back of his neck memorizing every inch of him pressed against me. The rough stubble of a five o'clock shadow, his hungry lips devouring mine, the hardening length digging into my stomach.

His free hand slid up my arm, and disentangled it. He pressed something hard and small into my palm before he finally let me go.

I studied the key with a frown. "What is it?"

He kissed me on the tip of the nose. "A house key."

"I know that, but why?"

He tugged me inside. Ryan was lounging against a nearby wall, arms crossed. "Why do you think?"

A hopeful bubble rose inside me. I didn't want to want this, or assume it was what I thought, but I couldn't help it. Still, this was one thing I was going to make them spell out. "You're going out of town, and you want me to water the plants?"

"You know that's not what it is," Seth said.

"Maybe." I couldn't fight my smirk, and my giddiness threatened to break loose. "But pretend I really am that dim."

Ryan kicked away from the wall, spinning to face me completely. "Even if you weren't having problems with your landlord—"

"That was between us." I shot a glare at Seth

"No." Seth shook his head. "We're not playing things that way. No more secrets."

"What he said." Ryan slipped a hand into Seth's back pocket. "And anyway. Even if it weren't the case, we don't want you to have to go home at night. Any night. I mean, obviously, you have to be okay with it, and pride isn't a good reason to say no. We'll all split the rent and such, so that's not even a valid excuse."

They'd already taken the wind out of my objections, and I had to admit, I didn't like the idea of going home at night either. "I'd love to."

It occurred to me, they were being awfully affectionate, with each other and with me, considering there would be a small crowd of people in the house soon. I felt a tug of relief we were going to be open about this. I didn't know how we were going to explain it, but I also didn't like the idea of hiding it.

Speaking of, where were all the other people? I glanced around the living room, realization sinking in. "There's no game tonight, is there?"

Seth gave Ryan a thoughtful look before turning back to me. "I don't know. We could role play *something* if you wanted."

Ryan nodded. "Locking the princess in the dungeon, for instance."

My cheeks warmed and anticipation spread through me. "Then rescuing her?"

Ryan seemed to consider this for a moment. "Probably eventually. I'll only keep her in chains until she's spent."

I liked the sound of that. Being bound and at his mercy.

"Hey," Seth interrupted. "Sometimes the innkeeper is going to want to be chained up too. This is only *mostly* about the princess."

His implication made me laugh, and added a new

layer of fantasy to the growing list of possibilities in my head. I was really looking forward to what the future held for us. "Druid," I corrected them. "She's a druid."

www.ingramcontent.com/pod-product-compliance
Lightning Source LLC
LaVergne TN
LVHW050937080826
845145LV00004B/1297